AMIRI & ODETTE

a LOVE Story

a poem by

WALTER DEAN MYERS

paintings by

JAVAKA STEPTOE

SCHOLASTIC PRESS
NEW YORK

Library of Congress Cataloging-in-Publication Data

Myers, Walter Dean, 1937-
Amiri and Odette : a dance for two / Walter Dean Myers ; paintings by Javaka Steptoe. —1st ed.
p. cm.

Summary: Presents a modern, urban retelling in verse of the ballet in which brave Amiri falls in love with beautiful Odette and fights evil Big Red for her on the streets of the Swan Lake Projects.

[1. Novels in verse. 2. Love—Fiction. 3. African Americans—Fiction. 4. Ballets—Stories, plots, etc. 5. Fairy tales.] I. Tchaikovsky, Peter Ilich, 1840-1893. Lebedinoe ozero. II. Steptoe, Javaka, 1971- ill. III. Title.
PZ7.5.M94Ami 2009
[Fic]—dc22
2008011563
ISBN-13: 978-0-590-68041-7
ISBN-10: 0-590-68041-2

Printed in Singapore 46

First edition, January 2009
The text type was set in Asphaltum WF & Gothic 13.
Book design by Phil Falco

For Miriam Altshuler, my Buddy
-WDM

This book is dedicated to the
love we have lost for ourselves.
Let it shine through.
-JS

HOW I CAME TO WRITE THIS POEM

Good stories are told and retold. The legend of the beautiful princess magically turned into a swan is part of Celtic, Russian, Slavic, and Arabian folklore. The stories always involve love, the vulnerability of the princess, and the possibility of her rescue. I had seen the ballet of *Swan Lake* as a child but it was as an adult, when I saw a production featuring Erik Bruhn, that I first noticed how significant a part the ever-present threat of violence played. This juxtaposition of great beauty and grace with a backdrop of pure evil stayed with me for years. As a writer, I absorb stories, allow them to churn within my own head and heart – often for years – until I find a way of telling them that fits both my time and temperament.

In listening to Pyotr Tchaikovsky's score, I found the violence muted, but slowly, in my head, the sometimes jarring rhythms of modern jazz and hip-hop began to intervene. I asked myself if there were modern dangers to young people similar to the magic spells of folklore. The answer, of course, was a resounding yes, and I began to craft a modern, urban retelling of the *Swan Lake* ballet.

Walking past a red brick housing development, I could sense the tensions that filled the corridors and alleys between the buildings. A few moments in front of the hard-topped basketball court revealed young basketball players, their bodies as taut and agile as any of the dancers I had seen on stage.

Here was the city, teeming with life, alive with the ever-present promise of youth. And yet I knew from the headlines that not all of these young people would be safe, that there were dangers lurking on every corner and in every shadow.

In *Swan Lake* the mother of the prince is worried about her son. She wants him to settle down, to lead a safe life. She offers him a party and a chance to choose a wife, and he agrees. The prince and his friends go into the woods and we learn that they are armed. We think their weapons will also keep them safe. But when the evil Rothbart appears, the traditional weapons are useless, and we are left hoping that there is sufficient strength within the young lovers to help them survive.

I believe in Amiri and Odette. I believe in the beauty of the music they hear and in the strength of their love. I believe in the mother who protects her son, and the friends who come to the party to celebrate Amiri's coming-of-age. In the retelling of this beautiful tale, I also believe in the magic of story to both heal and caution.

WALTER DEAN MYERS

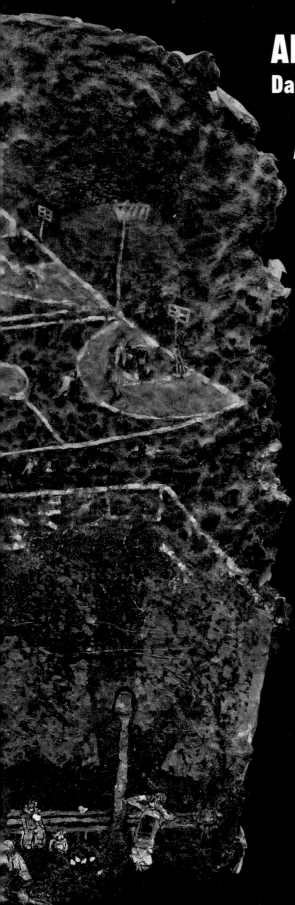

Above:
Dark clouds drift across a starless sky
And streak the fat, doom-heavy moon.

A distant thunder growls in sullen discontent
Like some evil beast awoke too soon.

Below:
The Swan Lake Projects crouch,
A twisted maze of asphalt truth.

An anxious mother feels the fearsome wind
And calls a warning to a troubled youth.

"THESE STREETS ARE VICIOUS.

THESE STREETS ARE WILD.

THESE STREETS HAVE MOUTHS.

They'll eat you, child!

"I've lived these projects
And know these things.
I've felt the fear when the doorbell rings.
You need to get settled, in a life that's straight,
With a wife and a family, before it's too late!
I'll throw you a party.
It'll be very select.
Boys from good families,
girls with respect.

But the boy is young, and his vision is bright.
He hasn't failed yet,
And thinks she forgets
That he is a warrior,
the Prince of the Night.

Amiri and Benny go down to the park,
Where a row of floodlights pushes back the dark.
Amiri's laces are tied, his eyes are radar beams,
They call it a game, but it's more than it seems.
"I take the ball up
With fingers as brown
As the round ball itself
Then SLAM it down.

ACT II

"BALL AGAINST CONCRETE
BALL AGAINST STEEL
BALL AGAINST HURTING
DO YOU KNOW HOW I FEEL?

This is my game, this is my world.
This is my passion, my talents unfurled.
On the court everything's right
For Amiri this night."

But on the far edge of this boy-boy dream,
As far as forever, as close as a scream,
There are girl shadows dancing
And one who is glancing

At the muscular form that leaps
toward the rim.
He sees her – she sees him.
A feeling of magic in the air.

He holds his breath,
she smooths her hair.

"How do they dance like that?"
Amiri speaks the words.
"So humanlike, yet like a flock
of troubled birds.
For just one minute I'll leave the game.

THERE'S ONE
SPECIAL GIRL.

I MUST DISCOVER
HER NAME."

The girl watches as Amiri draws near.
Her heart beats faster and yet there is fear.
She wants him to speak, to sing. . . .
But would he find her weak? A piteous thing?
When he looks, what will he see?
Her thin arms flutter nervously.

"Who are you?" she asks.
"Can you really be as fierce
As those dark eyes that seem to pierce
My very heart?"

"I AM AMIRI, THE PRINCE WHO SHAKES
IN YOUR PRESENCE.
YOU, WHOSE VOICE BREAKS LIKE
CRYSTAL AND WHOSE LOVELY BODY
SINGS OF SUNRISE
and all those magic things
That lift and swell and cause my heart
To nearly stop and tender dreams to start,
I AM AMIRI."

Transfixed, she mixes the words
Quickly in her mind.
Rummaging in memory
The right words to find.

"I AM ODETTE!"
SHE CRIES.

"I HAVE DANCED WITH ANGELS AND SUNG WITH NIGHTINGALES. I HAVE FLOWN THROUGH CLEAR SKIES AND SWUM WITH WHISTLING WHALES.

But now, like a fallen sparrow
On a golden chain,
I'm forever bound in shadow,
A prisoner to my pain."

IN A
CLUTTERING, FLUTTERING,
FLURRY OF WINGS

The other girls take to the skies.
Odette slinks away, shrinks away, gathers her things
And quickly averts her eyes.

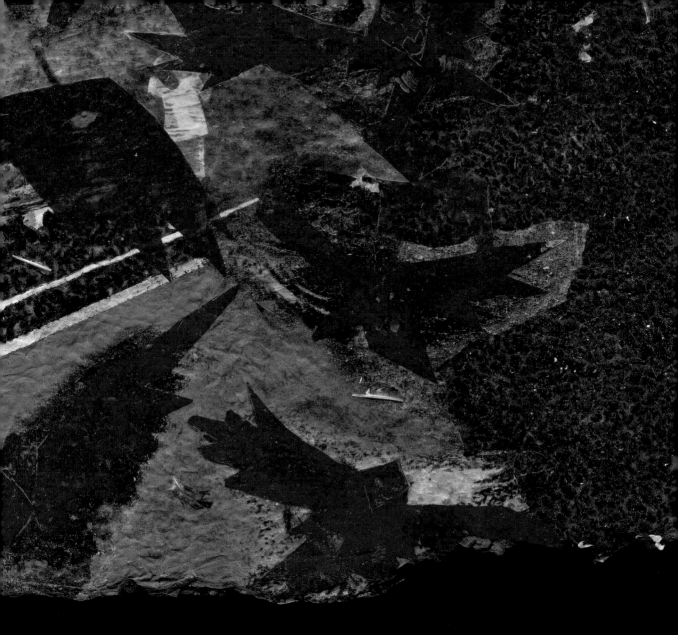

"YOU DON'T HAVE TO LEAVE,"
AMIRI PLEADS.

"My heart's on my sleeve. I'm someone who's needed

Just who you are, my princess, my star.

Give me one sign to convince

This lovesick and desperate prince."

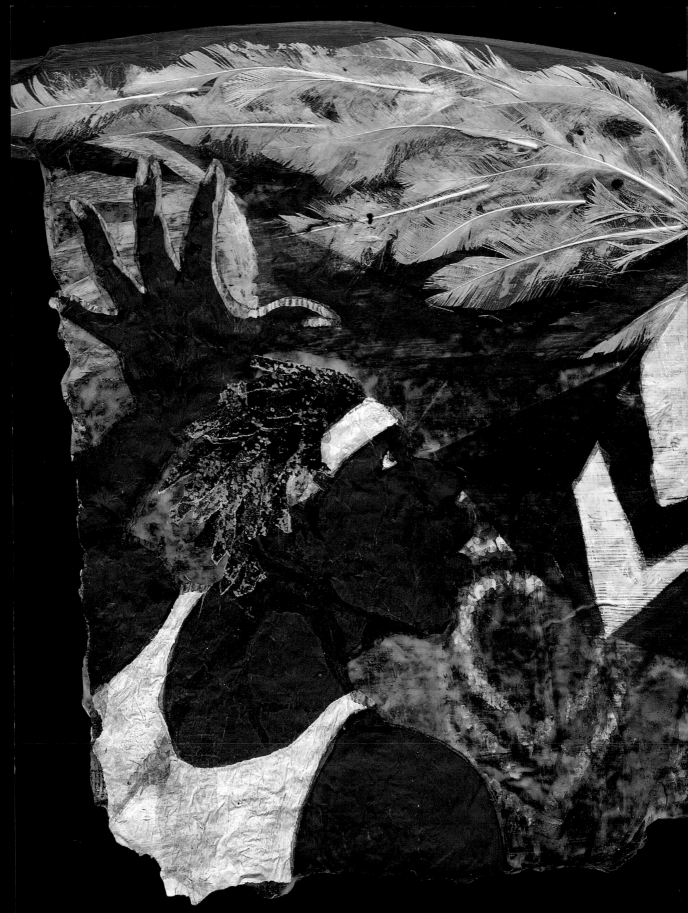

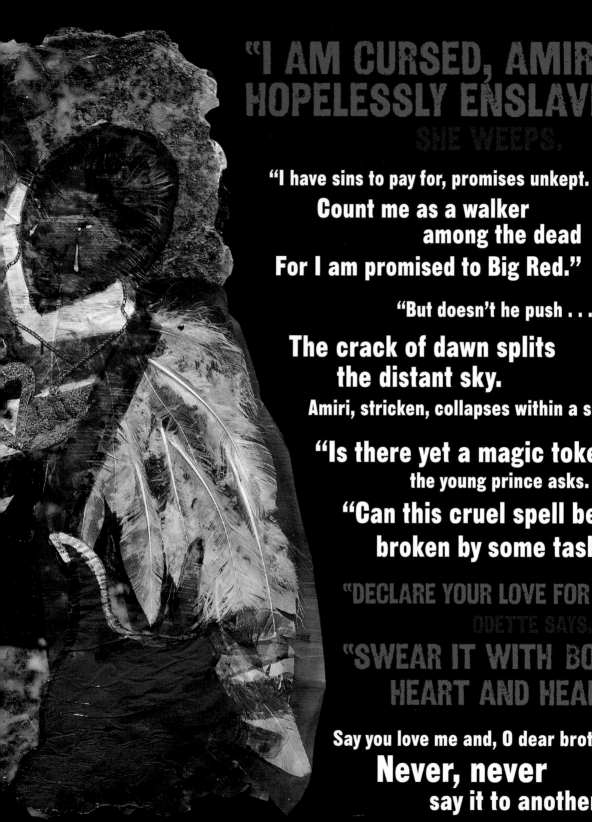

"I AM CURSED, AMIRI,
HOPELESSLY ENSLAVED,"
SHE WEEPS.

"I have sins to pay for, promises unkept.
Count me as a walker
among the dead
For I am promised to Big Red."

"But doesn't he push . . . ?"
The crack of dawn splits
the distant sky.
Amiri, stricken, collapses within a sigh.

"Is there yet a magic token?"
the young prince asks.
"Can this cruel spell be
broken by some task?"

"DECLARE YOUR LOVE FOR ME,"
ODETTE SAYS.
"SWEAR IT WITH BOTH
HEART AND HEAD.

Say you love me and, O dear brother,
Never, never
say it to another!"

"I LOVE YOU!"

AMIRI SAYS. "YOU, ODETTE, AND ONLY YOU!
YOU ARE THE ONE, AND THERE WILL NEVER BE A TWO.

My mom is giving a party.
It'll be eloquent and grand.

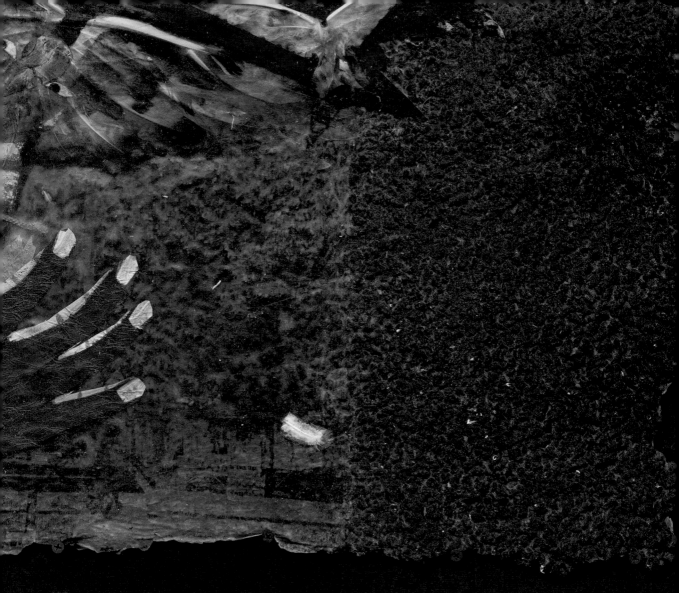

"Come, so she can meet you
And rejoice when I beg your hand."
And thus the pact is set, the bargain sealed,
Both agony and love revealed.
But are solutions so easily discovered?
Happy endings so readily recovered
Among the castaways and rejects
Of the teeming Swan Lake Projects?
Is happy chance alone gladly greeted
And Big Red so easily defeated?

Amiri's party is swinging and noisy,
Very girlsie and very boysie.
Thumping/bumping hot sweat jumping,
From muscle to hustle and back again.
But Amiri's smile hangs loosely on his face,
Lacking fire, void of grace.
Where is Odette, the girl he met?
He runs his fingers through his dreads, and sighs
As if something deep within has died.

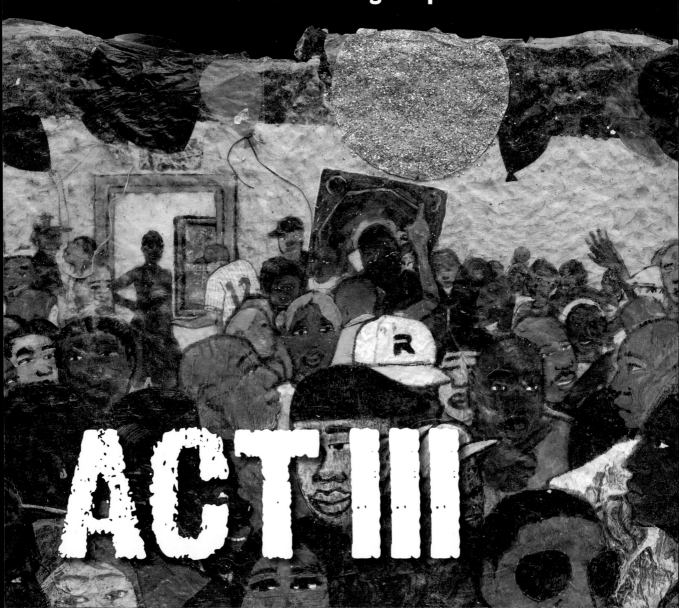

ACT III

"YO, AMIRI! COME ON! IT'S TIME TO GET DOWN!
WAY PAST THE MOMENT TO BE RID OF THAT FROWN!
AND WHO'S THAT GIRL WITH THE BLACK SWAN MASK?
SHE'S SO FINE, I'M SCARED TO ASK!"

Amiri turns and sees the girl,
Sees the lights around her swirl.
He is sure it is his love,
And yet . . .

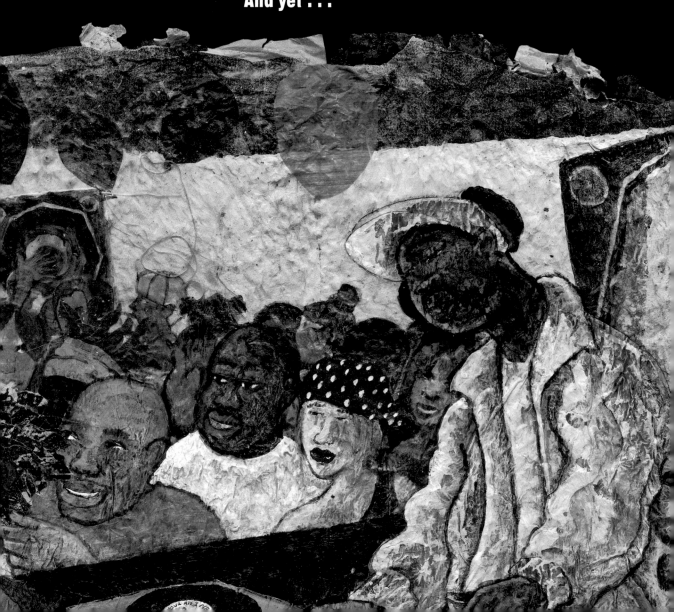

"ODETTE!" HE CALLS.

"AMIRI!" SHE RESPONDS.

She pulls him with a stunning glance
Across the crowded floor.
Until kiss-close they begin the dance
That will flame his heart once more.
They dance like mist on water,
As light as summer breeze.
He touches her waist — she kisses his cheek.
Her eyes begin to tease.
They dance like salsa angels.
They cling like summer vines.
He begs for more —
she moves away.

"ODETTE, WILL YOU BE MINE?"

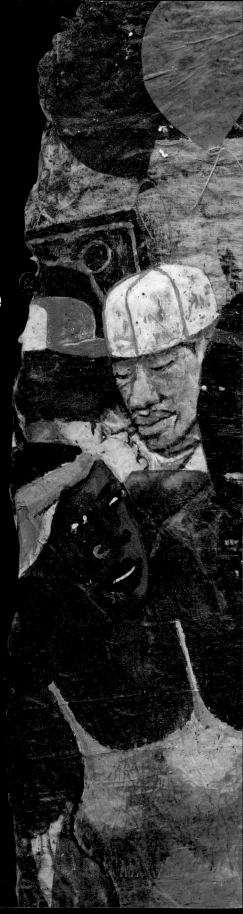

"WHAT ARE YOU SAYING?"

she asks, still masked,
still twirling about the floor.

"WHAT MUST I KNOW?"

"THAT I LOVE YOU!"

he calls, enthralled,
hoping for forevermore.

"I LOVE YOU SO!"

Reflected in the chandelier
Is Big Red's hand and nasty leer,
His hard lips in an evil curl.

It was he who had sent the girl —
the evil twin who played the part

That was to break Amiri's Heart.

From a corner it comes.

A SHRIEK! A WAIL!

A CRY THAT SAILS AGAINST THE PAINT-CRACKED WALLS.

A pitiful scream.
A citiful scream.

A pane-shattering scream.

A scream-scattering pain

That echoes down the halls of the Swan Lake Projects.

Amiri turns back to the girl
He thinks is his sweet love
Who has landed in the Swan Lake Projects
From the heavens far above.

In a moment sharpened with regret,
He knows he has betrayed Odette!
O muffle the drum and mute the horn,
From love's demise, despair is born!

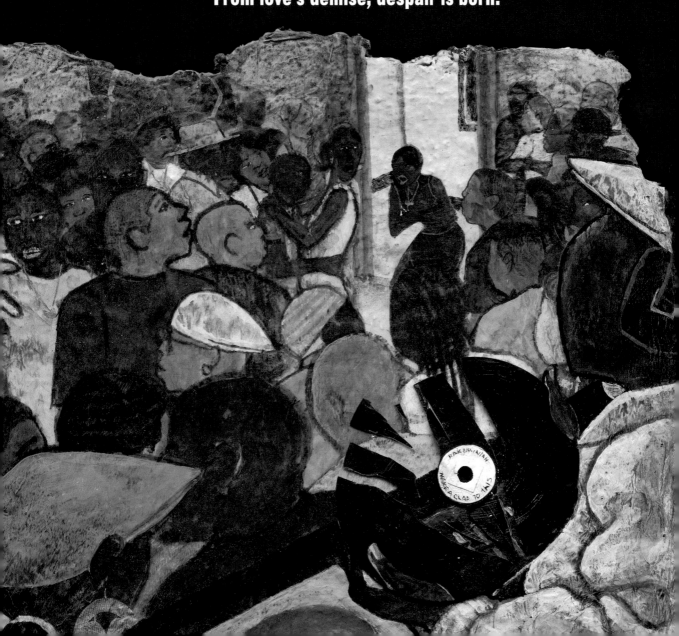

ACT IV

Amiri finds his love alone,
   shivering in the dark,
A broken arrow,
   quivering in that stark place where
she first gave meaning to his life,
Where he first thought that
   he had found a wife.

"Come with me, I will save you
   from Big Red," Amiri says.
"Go away, your Odette is already dead,"
   she answers. "You see a ghost, a specter
   wrapped in sorrow."

"No, I am Amiri," he says.
   "And what I see is a sweet promise of tomorrow.
Invent our love, and
   we will beat Big Red.
Without this hope, we might as well be dead."

"I OWN HER!"

BIG RED'S VOICE BOOMS IN THE EMPTY AIR.

"AND SHE NEEDS ME TO
   FEED HER FOUL DESPAIR!"

"No, no!"
Odette's wails nearly tear her soul apart,
As they wrench their way from her desperate heart.

"Amiri, be my man!
   Save me if you can!
If not, let my last pure breath
   Pledge my love to you in wretched death."

Evil laughter echoes
 Down the mocking streets,
Past the blues and painful dues,
 Down the tortured avenues
 Of the Swan Lake Projects.

"I CHOOSE AMIRI!"
ODETTE CALLS.

"WRITE *RIP* ON THE HANDBALL
WALLS IF YOU MUST
BUT ONLY TRUST
THAT THIS DAY
A DYING SWAN CHOSE
LOVE
AS HER ONLY WAY!"

Big Red is far from done.
There is a knife, there is a gun.
As cold steel flashes, a sharp blade slashes
Through the dark and steamy night.
With taut muscles and straining breath

AMIRI FACES GRINNING DEATH.
HIS EYES WILDLY GLEAMING,

HIS THROAT HOARSELY SCREAMING,
HE FIGHTS A DESPERATE FIGHT.

A twist of wrist, a swinging fist,
a cracking bone, a sudden groan.
One man is falling!
Now he is crawling
From the park and out of sight.
So Big Red at last is beaten down.
There is a stench as he slinks from town.

A fight for three so vicious,
        A victory for love delicious.

In its taste, its scent,
        Its sweet hope for the innocent,

A fight for three, a dance for two.
        Two hearts swirling through rare space,

Two bodies whirling to a place
        Big Red cannot go,

Where joy lives in spite of sorrow
        And gladness now denies tomorrow,

THEY DANCED. . . .

Amiri and Odette,

A dance for two, two dance as one,

Two bodies rising toward the sun

O sing, O sing, O sing

Of brave Amiri and beautiful Odette,

Of a time when love and evil met,

Then through the haze of simmer/summer days

There is a park which still echoes bouncing balls,
And the glad sound of lovers

Still echoes sweetly from the project walls.

ARTIST'S NOTE:

Amiri & Odette is a haunting story. I was struck by this poem that reminds readers that love does survive among the drug deals and gang violence of the inner city. In preparing the artwork, I want the reader to feel the grit, noise and urgency of the streets. The images are rendered with acrylic paint on slabs of asphalt, some of them as large as three feet wide. I have embellished the collages with candy wrappers, gold plated and 14k jewelry, newspaper, plastic bags and other items to give them a three-dimensional quality.

JAVAKA STEPTOE

ACKNOWLEDGMENTS:

Dancers such as Alvin Ailey, Arthur Mitchell, Eleo Pomare, and Bill T. Jones demonstrated that the classical arts could be brought into the urban arena to great effect. To these artists I am eternally grateful.

WALTER DEAN MYERS